Our Four Walls

by Carlynn Trout
illustrated by Phyllis Harris

 HOUGHTON MIFFLIN   BOSTON

My name is Emilio. Everybody knows me at the senior center. Abuela and I go there twice a week. We make people happy by reading aloud to them.

One rainy day, everyone was very bored when we arrived. The walls in the large meeting room were bare and plain looking.

"Abuela," I whispered, tugging at her sleeve. "I think I know a way to make everyone more cheerful."

Abuela smiled at me. She knows what a good thinker I am. She calls me her "smart nieto."

"Attention," she announced. "My smart nieto has an idea."

Everyone turned to look at me. I felt nervous, but I talked anyway. "These walls need some pictures," I said.

Everyone agreed.

Then Mrs. Luong, the oldest lady at the center, spoke up. "Yes. We need big ones so we can see them."

That gave me another really good idea.

Two days later, Abuela and I hurried to the center. Our arms were loaded with paints and paintbrushes.

"Let's get started," I said cheerfully as I entered the room.

"Aren't you going to read to us?" Mrs. Luong asked, surprised.

"Not today," I replied. "Today we're
painting."

"And we need your help," said Abuela,
handing out smocks. "We're going to make this
room more cheerful."

"That sounds like fun!" said Mrs. Luong.

Then I put my really good idea into action.

On one wall I wrote "ANIMALS" in capital letters. On another "PEOPLE." On a third "PLACES," and on a fourth "THINGS TO DO."

"Let the painting begin!" I cheered. "Choose any wall and paint something that matches the label."

Mrs. Green grabbed a paintbrush and rushed over to the ANIMALS wall. "I'll paint my dog, Scruffles," she said. "He's my sweetie."

Mr. Epstein joined her. "I'm going to paint my cat Queenie with a crown on her head!"

Mr. Chang started a picture of his three daughters on the PEOPLE wall. Mrs. Fox surprised everyone with a life-size portrait of herself.

"It's me!" she said, proudly.

On the PLACES wall, Mr. Andrews created a whole subway station. He even painted the token booth.

Abuela and I painted too. On the THINGS TO DO wall, we painted a picture of the two of us reading aloud.

Our Four Walls

When the walls were filled with colorful pictures, we threw a party. The director of the center hung up a special plaque.

Abuela and I still read at the center. Only now, it's not just the stories we're reading that make people happy. The beautiful walls make everyone happy too.